MABEL takes the FERRY

MABEL takes the FERRY

Emily Chetkowski (based on a true story)

illustrated by Dawn Peterson

Islandport Press, Inc.
P. O. Box 10
Yarmouth, Maine 04096
www.islandportpress.com

ISLANDPORT PRESS

Library of Congress Cataloging-in-Publication Data
Chetkowski, Emily.
  Mabel takes the ferry / by Emily Chetkowski; illustrated by Dawn Peterson.
    p. cm.
Summary: A fictionalized account of a mixed-breed dog's day of adventure
while searching for her family, who left her behind to go sailing on Penobscot Bay,
as she makes new friends on a ferry, at the beach, and in a
restaurant.

ISBN: 978-1-934031-99-5

1. Dogs—Juvenile fiction. [1. Dogs—Fiction. 2. Penobscot Bay (Me.)—Fiction.
3. Sailing—Fiction. 4. Maine—Fiction.] I. Peterson, Dawn, ill. II. Title.

PZ10.3.C4165Maf2001
[Fic}—dc21   2001046427   5431

Printed in Canada

With love to Marek and Hannah,
and of course Mabel

E.L.C.

A steady ocean breeze was blowing across Penobscot Bay, making it a most pleasant day on the island of Islesboro. An island dog and sailor at heart, Mabel could hardly contain her excitement as she watched her family packing for a day of sailing on their sloop *Off Call*. They hadn't taken her sailing yet this summer, and Mabel just knew today would be her turn to go.

No one was sure exactly what kind of dog Mabel was, but her shaggy fur, sad eyes, short legs and shiny black nose made everyone love her. It was no mystery where her love for sailing came from. Ever since her first dinghy ride when she was merely a pup, Mabel took to the sea as eagerly as her sailing family. On days like this, with a constant breeze and sparkling seas, sailing was the only thing on her mind. She loved the salty smell of the ocean and how the breeze made her floppy ears blow straight back.

"Oh no, not again!" thought Mabel as she watched her family drive off without her. Ever since little Hannah had arrived, no one seemed to notice Mabel. Even young Marek didn't play with her anymore. He was always playing with Hannah. No matter how hard she tried to get their attention, her tricks just didn't work. But Mabel knew they still loved her and she didn't give up hope.

"Maybe they just forgot me by mistake," she thought.
"If I hurry, I can catch them!"
So she set off running across the field and down the road toward Gilkey's Harbor, where *Off Call* was moored near the island ferry dock.

As she ran by a neighbor's house, they called out her name. "Hmm, bacon and eggs," thought Mabel as she stopped in her tracks and sniffed the air. But there was no time for breakfast today. She had to hurry.

Crossing the field in front of the old sea captain's house at the head of the harbor, Mabel glanced out at the water. The Flying Fish, an island schooner, was enjoying a freshening breeze and the sight of it spurred Mabel on.

At last she arrived at the dock, but only in time to see her family sailing off toward the Camden hills. Mabel was so disappointed and about to give up hope, when she noticed people lining up to board the ferry to the mainland.

"Maybe I can catch them on the ferry," she thought as she hurried over to get in line. Almost immediately the ferry horn sounded and everyone started to board, including Mabel. The timing was perfect. "I still have a chance!" Mabel was excited as she walked down the ramp.

Mabel followed a friendly group of people up to the bow. "They must be tourists," she thought as they petted her and took her picture. "I hope my fur doesn't look too windblown," she worried as she posed for the camera and gave a doggy smile.

From the bow, Mabel could see most of west Penobscot Bay. She saw seals and porpoises playing in the water, and even barked at a gull or two. But she didn't see her family among the many boats out sailing.

Mabel was the first to get off when the ferry docked at Lincolnville Beach. "Maybe they're here," she hoped as she headed down to the crowded beach.

Searching the crowd, Mabel made many new friends but couldn't find her family. "It's no use," thought Mabel and hung her head in sadness.

She started back to the ferry until she was surprised to find the ocean right at her paws. Mabel loved to swim and jumped right in! She fetched sticks that her new friends threw for her and spent most of the afternoon playing in the surf. It was a great day for the beach!

Before long, Mabel started to get hungry.
While having so much fun, she had lost all
track of time! "I guess I should have stopped
for bacon and eggs," she thought. Just then she
noticed the lobster restaurant so located right
there on the beach. The aroma of
lobster and steak led her up onto the
restaurant's deck.

At first hardly anyone noticed her. But that
didn't last long as Mabel made herself the
center of attention by performing tricks.
Her favorite, standing on her hind legs
and waving with her front paws, was a
real crowd pleaser. It wasn't long before she
was full of lobster and steak scraps, reward for
her fine performance.

In the distance, the ferry horn sounded—the *Margaret Chase Smith* was ready to depart. Startled, Mabel ran to the dock. But she was too late! The ferry had already left the pen, bound for Islesboro.

"I'll just wait right here for the next ferry," Mabel decided. She sat on the dock until almost dark, but the ferry never returned. It had been the last trip of the day.

Tired, scared, with nowhere else to go and no way to get home, Mabel returned to the restaurant. A waiter said, "She must be lost. I think I'll keep her." Mabel was really in a mess now! But the manager found her dog tags on her collar that were hidden by all her shaggy fur. He called her family, long since home from sailing. "Whew, that was a close call," sighed Mabel.

When they heard the news, Mabel's family said, "She's where? We were so worried about her! But because the ferry isn't running right now, we'll have to sail over to get her." So they packed up again and set sail for Lincolnville Beach.

By now it was dark, but the full moon that lit up the sky helped Mabel's family find their way and avoid a huge barge heading up the bay.

They docked the boat and hurried to the restaurant. When Mabel saw them she barked with joy, but she just wanted to go home. She ran down the beach and was the first to board the boat.

With Mabel as the look-out and her family at the helm, they followed the silvery path of moonlight on the water back home to Islesboro.

At last they were all together, and Mabel thought it was the best sail EVER!

About the Author

A native New Englander, Emily Chetkowski summers in Maine. She enjoys spending her time there boating, writing, and looking for her dog. She is the author of *Mabel Takes a Sail, Pumpkin Smile, Sister Sluggers,* and *Just a Kid.* When not in Maine, she lives on her farm in Massachusetts, writing and enjoying her many animals.

About the Dog

Mabel, a dog of no particular background, enjoys taking walks to visit her neighbors and swimming. She also enjoys boating rides in the car, eating the cat's food, and barking at nothing.

About the Artist

Dawn Peterson is a freelance artist and illustrator living on the coast of Maine.

photo by Winthrop, Inc.

Emily Chetkowski and Mabel.